The Animals' Football Final

by Clare De Marco and Trevor Dunton

First published in 2015 by
Franklin Watts
338 Euston Road
London
NW1 3BH

Franklin Watts Australia
Level 17/207 Kent Street
Sydney
NSW 2000

A CIP catalogue record for this book is available
from the British Library.

ISBN 978 1 4451 3878 7 (hbk)
ISBN 978 1 4451 3879 4 (pbk)
ISBN 978 1 4451 3884 8 (library ebook)
ISBN 978 1 4451 3883 1 (ebook)

Series Editor: Jackie Hamley
Series Advisor: Catherine Glavina
Series Designer: Peter Scoulding

Printed in China

Franklin Watts is a divison of
Hachette Children's Books,
an Hachette UK company.
www.hachette.co.uk

It was Cup Final Day.
Jungle United were
playing Amazon F.C.

But there was a problem.
Jungle United's bus
was stuck.

Jungle United fans waited and waited for their team.

"They're not coming," said Meerkat. "We'll have to play ourselves, or lose!"

Amazon FC burst out onto the pitch. Jaguar roared into attack.

Ananconda coiled around the goal and Crocodile snapped into defence.

The new Jungle United crept on. The dung beetles went in attack.

The meerkats went in midfield and defence and Porcupine went in goal.

The whistle blew. Jaguar scored straight away.

"1-0 to the Amazon!"

roared their fans.

Then the meerkats got the ball up the pitch.

The dung beetles pushed the ball with all their might.

Crocodile kept snapping to defend, but the ball wiggled away from him.

“GOAL for Jungle United!

1-1!”

Soon after, the dung beetles got the ball again.

Anaconda tried to save ...

... but the meerkats made her laugh.

"2-1 to Jungle United!"

The game was nearly over when the Jungle United bus arrived.

"We're winning!" roared Lion. "Keep going!"

JUNGLE UTD 2
AMAZON F.C. 1
HELLO MUM!

With seconds left, Jaguar took a brilliant shot ...

… then the ball popped.
“Sorry!” said Porcupine.

The whistle blew. "Three cheers for the new Jungle United!" cried the Jungle United team. "We're your biggest fans!"

Puzzle 1

Put these pictures in the correct order.
Now tell the story in your own words.
How short can you make the story?